GENIE AND TEENY

WISH UPON A STAR

ONCE UPON A WISH

Steven Lenton

HarperCollins *Children's Books*

First published in the United Kingdom by
HarperCollins *Children's Books* in 2023
HarperCollins *Children's Books* is a division of HarperCollins*Publishers* Ltd
1 London Bridge Street
London SE1 9GF

www.harpercollins.co.uk

HarperCollins*Publishers*
Macken House, 39/40 Mayor Street Upper
Dublin 1, D01 C9W8, Ireland

1

ISBN 978–0–00–840858–9

Steven Lenton asserts the moral right to be
identified as the author and illustrator of the work.

A CIP catalogue record for this title is available from the British Library.

Printed and bound in the UK using 100% renewable electricity at CPI Group (UK) Ltd

This book is produced from independently certified FSC™ paper
to ensure responsible forest management.

For more information visit: www.harpercollins.co.uk/green

If you cou... ...ke ...ee wishes,

what would Y... ...?

jot them d...wn here!

MY WISH LIST*

1 _____

_____

2 _____

_____

3 _____

_____

*YOU <u>CAN'T</u> WISH FOR MORE WISHES,
SO <u>DON'T</u> EVEN BOTHER TRYING!

Books by Steven Lenton

The Genie and Teeny books in reading order:

FOR PHIL TITE AND THE CHILDREN OF
EDWARD BRYANT SCHOOL. SL X

HELLO, READER!

It's so **nice** to see you again, especially after all the excitement of Genie and Teeny's last adventure! Do you remember, they had a funny old time in a theme park helping Grant get back home to WISHALUZIA?

There was a magic wishing well, silly sausages and a ride on the tallest roller coaster in the world!

After a successful mission, Tilly and Teeny went back home to Earth, and Grant returned safely to his family in the land of genies.

We join them now after a good night's sleep, at the breakfast table, where Grant's dad is making piles of **delicious** starberry pancakes . . .

CHAPTER 1
A MAGiCAL
BREAKFAST

'Extra sparkle syrup on mine, please, Dad!' Grant requested excitedly. 'It's so nice to be back. I do love Earth, but the breakfasts were a little, erm, boring – they have things like flakes made from corns and cross ants!'

'Urgh, gross!' Grant's sister Greta shouted, pulling a face. 'Earth sounds like a total nightmare.'

She gave her dad a big hug, then she and Grant did their special greeting – sticking their tongues out at each other, waggling their hands, touching elbows then flying round each other in a circle.

They all scoffed the huge
pile of starberry pancakes
and their dad did a

BIG

burp.

Greta followed

with a HUGE

burp, then Grant let rip a

GINORMOUS

burp that shook their
entire lamp-shaped
home. Then they all got

the giggles, which is funny because Grant's family name is Giggle.

Grant Giggle, Greta Giggle and Gregory Giggle, known collectively as **the Giggles**.

After half an hour, they all stopped giggling and Grant went to open the front door to go and explore WISHALUZIA, but his dad and Greta both shouted, 'GRANT, NO! STOP!'

Grant froze and Greta rushed to slam the door shut.

Grant's dad suddenly looked very serious . . .

CHAPTER 2
A RiGHT ROYAL PROBLEM

Grant's dad LOOKED very serious because he WAS being very serious, for a change.

'Grant, you can't just go wandering off like that. You're safe inside our home, but you are still banned from WISHALUZIA by

Queen Mizelda, remember?' Dad explained.

'Oh yes, I'd forgotten that bit!' replied Grant, taking a deep breath. 'It seems so long ago that the queen **mistook** me for the royal chef on her birthday, and wanted me to make her a birthday cake, but I turned her into a birthday snake by **mistake**, and she banished me from Genie World and I landed on Earth, found Teeny and Tilly, was captured by Lavinia Lavender, went to school with an alligator, got chased by Sidney Snoop and finally ended up back with you guys after riding the CRAZY CLOUD COASTER and falling into a wishing well!' Grant took another deep

breath after that very, very long sentence and sat back down at the kitchen table.

'You can't go out, Grant, or you'll get caught by the queen's royal guards. Look!' Greta pointed at the window as two guards wearing feathered helmets and red robes marched past. Grant ducked down until they had gone.

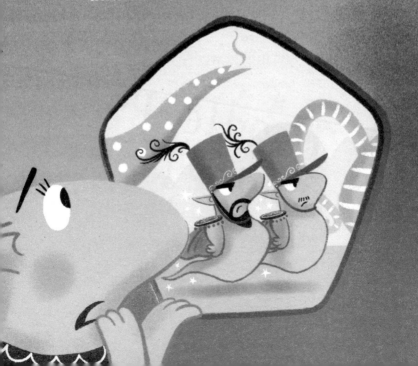

'But I can't stay in here all day. I'll go bonkers!' Grant sighed.

'So will we,' Dad whispered under his breath.

'I heard that, Dad!' Grant said, frowning.

'What we need is a plan!' Greta exclaimed. 'For starters, you'll need a disguise so you won't be recognised by anyone. What about something like this?' She clicked her fingers and said her magic wishy word:

'Poodle~parp~ a~pipsqueak!'

There was a cloud of *sparkly pink smoke*, and a pair of funny glasses, big floppy ears and a moustache appeared on Grant's face.

'Hmm, it's still obviously you,' Greta said disappointedly.

'How about this!' shouted their dad, clicking his fingers and saying his magic wishy word:

'Jim-a-jam-a-jumplebumps!'

There was a large plume of green sparkly smoke and, as the cloud cleared, Grant appeared, wearing a large white sheet with eyeholes cut into it, like a ghost.

'Dad! You can't

tell it's Grant, but I do think everyone in WISHALUZIA might wonder why a ghost is suddenly haunting them!' Greta giggled.

'Good point,' Dad replied.

'I have it!' Grant said with a twinkle in his eye. He flew up to his room and vanished inside his tea-lamp.

'Alaka-blam-a-bumwhistle!'

Then he reappeared downstairs with a **'TA-DAH!'** Greta screamed. 'It's a royal guard! **HELP!'**

'Calm down, Greta! It's me, Grant. I'm not actually a royal guard – I just remembered that I had a royal helmet in my hat collection. I knew it would come in handy one day.'

'Oh phew!' Greta sighed in relief.

But, before they could continue discussing the plan, there was a sudden knock at the door . . .

CHAPTER 3
GUARDS!

'**Oooh,** I hope it's the Postgenie!' Grant's
dad said with glee. 'I'm expecting a special
delivery!'

He opened the door, but it wasn't a special
delivery, unless his special delivery was . . .

'ACTUAL ROYAL GUARDS!' Greta squeaked.

Grant, still disguised as a royal guard himself, gulped.

'We need to speak with Mr Giggle!' one of the guards shouted.

'Er, I'm Mr Giggle, but please, you can call me Greg,' Grant's dad replied nervously.

'Er, I mean, thank you for letting me use your loo, Dad, er, Mr Giggle. I wouldn't go in there for five minutes, though, if I were you!' He laughed nervously.

'Guard, what are you doing here? And why is your uniform all wonky?' the other guard demanded.

Grant straightened his helmet and put on a deep voice. 'Ahem, I too was searching for Grant and have done a full search of this lamp and can confirm that there is no sign of him in here, so you can leave now. Thank you, bye-bye!' Grant waved.

Just then, the feather on his helmet tickled

his nose, making Grant s n e e z e.

The helmet flew into the air and he caught it and put it back on, but it was too late – the guards had realised who he was!

'Oi! You're not a guard – you're HIM! GRAB HIM!' they shouted.

They lurched forward, but just as they were about to capture Grant a **huge** shadow appeared over them and an

ENORMOUS

creature came down from the sky, gobbled the guards up and

flew away again.

Grant, Greta and their dad blinked in
disbelief, then ran outside to see what it was.

In the distance they saw what looked like a
giant cat creature with huge wings, a long
tail and, oddly, a *small* crown on its head.

Genies were running around, screaming, as the creature sᴡᴏᴏᴘᴇᴅ through ᴡɪsʜᴀʟᴜᴢɪᴀ, breathing fire, crashing into buildings and meow-roaring loudly. **It was chaos!**

CHAPTER 4
THE ROYAL RESCUE!

'What *is* that monster?' shouted Greta.

'Looks like an **enormous** flying cat

thing!' Grant replied among all the hubbub.

'And it seems to be heading to the palace!'

Sure enough, the monster was flying

towards the home of the queen, meow-roaring loudly as it soared high above WISHALUZIA.

'Guard, come with us! We must defend Her Majesty!' ordered another guard who, as he ran past, swept Grant up with the others.

'WAIT!' Greta shouted after him, but it was too late – Grant found himself being carried along with the other guards in the direction of the palace.

Grant was trying to keep quiet, but it was proving difficult – it was amazing to be inside the fancy-shmancy palace grounds.

'WOW, **shimmering** golden statues of the queen!' he observed.

'Oh . . .'

OUR QUEEN!

'WOW, beautiful bushes in the shape of the queen!

Oh . . .'
gulped Grant.

The guards were trying all manner of ways to fight the feline beast – some were **spraying** it with water, others were *firing* arrows, while yet more were attempting to use their Magic – but nothing seemed to be working. The cat monster was just too big!

'We're going to be burned alive – run for your lives!' all the guards screamed, crying and rushing away.

'Cowards!' shouted the queen, who had been observing everything from her bedroom window at the top of a tower when, at that moment, she caught sight of Grant, who was now hiding behind a burnt flag. 'You there! Guard genie! HELP ME!!!' cried Queen Mizelda, waving frantically at him.

Grant gulped again and floated up towards her.

The queen raised an eyebrow. 'Don't I know you from somewhere?' she asked, looking Grant up and down, and seeming highly suspicious.

'Er, no, Your Majesty. I've never seen you before in my life.'

At which point, the queen sneered and flared her nostrils in anger. 'Well, whoever you are, GET ME OUT OF HERE!' she screamed.

'Don't worry, Your Majesty, I will protect you!' Grant said, saluting. He took the queen's hand and led her out of the palace. They flew down the spiral stairs of the tower past beautifully ornate stained-glass windows.

But the cat monster saw them trying to escape! It flew towards them, roaring louder than ever, and shattered the windows with its huge tail.

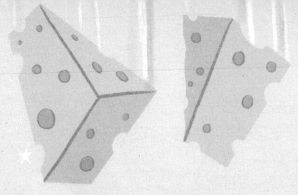

Grant and the queen flew as fast as they could through the halls of the palace as the beast smashed **more** walls and windows behind them.

Grant attempted some quick magic to get rid of the cat monster.

'Alaka-blam-a-buMwhistle!

. . . erm . . .

FREEZE!'

But the big cat didn't freeze. Instead,
a load of CHEESE fell from the sky on
to the monster, who gobbled it all up and
then carried on chasing them. Grant tried
something else.

'Alaka-blaM-a-buMwhistle!

. . . erm . . . **SHRINK!**'

But the big cat didn't shrink. Instead, a drink of milk appeared in the monster's claws, which it drank, before it licked its lips, meowed in delight, then carried on chasing Grant and the queen. Grant had one more try.

'Alaka-blaM-a-buMwhistle!

erm . . .

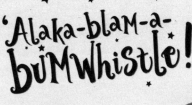

SKATEBOARD!'

And a skateboard appeared underneath

the beast.

'Whoa!'

Wobble,

whoosh!

The cat lost its balance, flailing its paws and wings. But then it seemed to get quite used to the skateboard and started doing flips and tricks, speeding up and getting ever closer to them!

'YIKES, sorry!' Grant shouted to the queen. 'I'm all out of ideas!'

'It's you!' the queen shrieked. 'You're that despicable genie who turned me into a birthday snake! I'd recognise that terrible magic anywhere. Guards – capture him and take him to the dungeons!' Then it dawned on her. 'Ah yes, there are no guards, except YOU!' She sighed.

'Wait!' said Grant excitedly, and they both stopped and hid behind a pillar. 'Did you say DUNGEONS?!' he asked, out of breath.

'Yes, of course I did. Every queen has a dungeon – where else are we supposed to put naughty genies like you?!' she snapped.

'Ahem, Earth?' Grant whispered to himself.

'WHAT?' said the queen.

'Er, nothing. Let's go down to the dungeons. We'll be safe there for a while and we can come up with a plan,' Grant suggested.

The queen sneered at first, but then nodded.

'What choice do I have? It's down these stairs. Follow me . . .'

CHAPTER 5

TO THE DUNGEONS!

The queen led Grant down another set of
spiral stairs to a series of dark gated rooms.
'**OPEN!**' she commanded and the
gates of one of the cells flew open and
they rushed into a gloomy space, lit only

by burning torches. **'CLOSE!'** she shouted quickly as soon as they were inside. The gates slammed shut. There was nothing in the dungeon cell except for lots of cobwebs and a very battered dusty old lamp in the corner.

They were both really out of breath, but they managed to breathe a sigh of relief.

'Phew! I think we lost it!' Grant huffed.

But, just as he said it, the cat monster's huge eyeball appeared at the bars of the dungeon window and meow-roared angrily. Dust fell from the ceiling and a frightened spider scuttled away.

'Okay, Your Majesty, I think I have a plan to

get rid of the cat monster, but do you have

any idea why it's after you?' Grant asked.

'None at all. He's just a stupid big old smelly thing with nothing better to do, I suppose,' she said.

'How do you know it's a he-cat?' Grant was puzzled.

'Oh, er, I don't know – I'm just guessing. I find most he-things are big and smelly,' she snapped.

'Well, I think you're safe here for a while, so I'm going home to put a plan into action,' Grant said with determination.

'Wait! You can't just leave me here with that thing!' the queen squealed, pointing at the big eyeball.

But Grant had already vanished from the dungeons and was heading home.

CHAPTER 6
A CUNNiNG PLAN!

'You're back!' exclaimed Greta and Dad as a very out-of-puff Grant reappeared inside their lamp.

He gave them a rundown of everything that had just happened back at the palace.

'WOW, Grant! That's incredible – we were so worried! We started to come after you but got trampled by all the queen's guards and decided it was best to wait here for you,' Greta explained.

'No time to lose – I have an idea!' said Grant. 'So . . . the creature wrecking WISHALUZIA is basically a massive cat with wings. Teeny the dog LOVES to chase cats back on Earth and he can smell them a mile off! We need to bring Teeny back here, turn him into a dog monster and then he can chase the cat monster away! TO THE MAGIC MIRROR!' he exclaimed excitedly.

The three genies ran up to Grant's bedroom and stood in front of a large, ornate magic mirror next to his bed. The mirror was linked to the smaller mirror that Grant had given Tilly and Teeny in case they needed each other.

'Tilly! Teeny! Are you there?' Grant shouted into it.

Nothing happened.

Grant tapped the mirror. 'Is this thing on?!' he asked.

'Try switching it off and on again,' his dad
suggested.

Grant clicked a little button on the back of the
mirror and then a blurry image came into view.

'It worked!' said Greta.

'Tilly, is that you? You look a bit hairier
than the last time we saw you!' Grant said,
squinting.

'Woof!' replied Teeny.

The genies chuckled.

'Teeny! It's you! How have you been, fella?
Is Tilly there?' Greta asked.

Teeny shook his head and pointed at the
school calendar on the wall.

'Oh no.

Is Tilly at school?' said Grant.

He turned to his dad and sister. 'I

went there once. It was a LOT of fun, but I'd

avoid the boys' toilets!'

Teeny shuddered, remembering the strange

events that had occurred on Bring Your Pet to

School Day.

'Well, as it happens, Teeny, it's YOUR help we really need! A mysterious, gigantic cat monster is attacking WISHALUZIA and we think you are just the dog to chase it away! What do you reckon?' Grant asked.

Teeny gulped and hid under a pillow.

'It'll be okay, Teeny. We'll help you!' Dad reassured him.

The pillow began to shake just as Grant clicked his fingers and said his magic wishy word,

'Alaka-blam-a-bumwhistle!'

There was a flash of sparkly turquoise smoke, the mirror rose into the air and started to spin in the middle of the room, then the glass in it swirled *faster* and *faster*.

Suddenly a very waggy tail appeared,
followed by a brown furry bottom, furry legs
and finally the rest of . . .

'TEENY, you're here!' Grant gave him a huge
hug and Teeny licked Grant's face.

'Welcome back, Teeny!' Greta and her dad
chanted.

CHAPTER 7

TURNING TEENY!

'I'll put the kettle on!' said Dad.

'I don't think it will fit!' giggled Greta as they both flew down the stairs.

'Stop it, you two. There's no time for tea! We have to save WISHALUZIA!' Grant said seriously.

They gathered round the kitchen table and, remembering when Tilly sketched a plan to help him get back home, Grant pointed his finger in the air. Magical sparkles appeared from it and he started to draw.

'Okay, the cat monster is hanging round the palace, trying to eat Queen Mizelda—' Grant started.

'Oh, so it's not all bad, then,' Greta interrupted with a smirk.

'Greta!' Dad scolded.

Grant continued as his magical plan appeared magically before them. 'We need to turn Teeny into a dog monster, then ride him to the palace **HERE** and chase away the cat monster who is hovering near the dungeons **HERE**. Hopefully, Monster Teeny will scare him so much he'll never come back!' Grant laughed.

The plan hung, sparkling, in the air as they studied it.

'Sounds good to me, son!' Dad smiled.

'Now to turn Teeny into Monster Teeny!' Greta said, clapping with excitement.

Grant picked up Teeny and placed him on a chair.

'Okay, here goes. Let's turn Teeny into a **MONSTER DOG!'** said Grant, twiddling his nose, wiggling his ears and fingers and uttering his magic wishy word:

'Alaka-blam-a-bumwhistle!'

There was a loud whooshing noise, lots of sparkly turquoise smoke and . . .

'GRANT! I thought you said monster DOG not monster LOG!' Greta giggled.

Indeed! Grant had transformed Teeny into a HUGE wooden log and not only that, but it had filled the entire lamp!

The log blinked and looked nervous.

'I think we need to take this outside! Let me have a go,' said Dad as the three genies squeezed out of the back door of the lamp. He waved his hands and shouted his magic wishy word:

'Jim-a-jam-a-jumplebumps!'

There was a huge plume of green sparkly smoke, and the log disappeared from inside the lamp, then in the back garden there appeared . . .

'DAD!' Grant and Greta exclaimed. 'You've turned him into a monster FROG!'

'*RIBBIT!*' Teeny croaked.

'Oops, sorry, Teeny!' Dad apologised, his cheeks turning pink with embarrassment.

Frog Teeny's long tongue started flicking out to catch a nearby fly.

'Okay, you two, it's my turn. Let me show you how it's done!' Greta spun round in a circle, waggled her hands and said her magic

wishy word: **'Poodle~parp~ a~pipsqueak!'**

There was an enormous cloud of pink

sparkly smoke and . . .

'Oh, Greta, you've really done it this time!'

Grant exclaimed.

Greta stood with her eyes closed, looking

really pleased with herself.

'Yep,' Dad agreed, 'you've REALLY done it this time!' He giggled.

Greta opened her eyes to see her triumphant Teeny transformation, but . . .

'OH NO! Teeny, I've turned you into a **GIANT HOG!** I'm so sorry!'

'OINK!' oinked Teeny.

'Right, we can't waste any more time – we need to focus. Let's all try together!' Grant suggested.

Greta and Dad nodded and Hog-Teeny grunted.

They all closed their eyes and combined their magic wishy words, shouting:

'Alaka-parp-a-jumpwhistle!'

and clouds of turquoise, green and pink sparkly smoke surrounded Hog-Teeny, then disappeared to reveal . . .

Teeny, towering above them with huge wings, a long dragonlike tail, sharp teeth and big scaly ears.

'YAY, WE DID IT!
Teeny, you're a **MONSTER!**'
they all shouted.

CHAPTER 8
HOW TO TRAIN YOUR TEENY!

'AWESOME!' said Greta. 'Let's call him

Tyranno-Teeny!'

Teeny stood to attention, but then he

fell over on his wobbly legs. The three

genies flew out of the way to avoid getting

squashed. Teeny wasn't quite used to his new body yet . . .

'I think Tyranno-Teeny needs some training before he's ready to rescue the queen! And it will have to be some pretty intensive training. We don't have long!' stated Grant.

The three genies got to work. Grant nipped into his tea-lamp and grabbed a whistle and three sweatbands from his hat collection, giving one to his dad and one to his sister. Then they all put them on their heads.

'Dad, you're in charge of flying training . . .'

Grant's dad saluted.

'Greta, you're in charge of roaring

training . . .' Greta saluted.

'And I will be in charge of fire-breathing training!' Grant finished, saluting himself.

'Let's do this!' they all said together.

'GULP!' gulped Tyranno-Teeny.

Grant blew his whistle.

'Let the training begin!' he shouted.

Dad showed Teeny how to spread his wings and flap them, but Teeny wasn't quite getting the hang of it.

Reader, maybe you can help them? Hold
this book open in half, like a bird, and move
it up and down so the pages either side of the
spine flap like wings . . .

BRILLIANT! It worked! Teeny can fly perfectly now. Well done, reader!

Next, Dad showed Teeny how to loop-the-loop and barrel-roll . . .

. . . which Teeny eventually got the hang of!

Then Greta attempted to show Teeny how to roar. She showed him how to take a deep breath in, how to open his mouth as wide as he could and how to shout as loudly as possible . . .

But only a tiny 'woof' sound came out of his giant mouth.

He tried again, but this time, instead of a woof, he did a little burp instead.

Reader, maybe you can help show Teeny how to do a really loud and scary roar?

After three, I want to hear the loudest, scariest roar you can muster. Ready?

One, two, three . . .

ROOOOOO OOOAAAAAAAAAAA AARRRRRRRRR!

WOW! That was much better, Teeny. Thank you, reader – you did it again!

Now it was Grant's turn to train Tyranno-Teeny how to breathe fire, which was going to be difficult because Grant didn't actually know how to breathe fire himself.

Grant grabbed his Thinking Cap from his tea-lamp, put it on and had a good think. AHA! He remembered a time when he played a joke on his dad and put too much hot sauce on his food till it made him do fiery hiccups!

He flew to the kitchen, fried a big pile of sausages, then found the big bottle of hot sauce in the cupboard. Quick as a flash, he poured it all over the sausages and took them outside to Teeny.

Tyranno-Teeny's eyes widened with joy when he saw the huge plate of bangers. He licked his lips and tucked in, gobbling the lot in seconds.

Grant, Greta and their dad looked at Teeny and waited for the hiccups.

They waited.

And waited . . . but nothing happened.

'What are we going to do now?' Greta asked Grant.

But, before he could answer her, they heard a rumbling sound that got **louder** and **louder** and **LOUDER.**

'It's coming from Teeny's tummy!' Dad shouted. 'Quick, get down!'

The three genies threw themselves on the ground, covered their heads and watched. But no fire came out of Teeny's mouth . . . Instead, there was a very loud $PARP$ and a huge jet of flame came out of another part of Teeny's body!

Teeny looked very embarrassed.

'Well, that's one way to breathe fire!' chuckled Dad.

Teeny gave another little PARP and singed a passing bird.

'We don't have any more time – that will have to be TRAINING COMPLETE!' Grant exclaimed. *Let's go!*

CHAPTER 9
TO THE PALACE!

Grant, Greta and their dad jumped on to Tyranno-Teeny's back, ready for take-off. He started to run forward as he flapped his wings, then WHOOSH! They were up in the air!

'WOW! Look at the view!' Greta
shouted in amazement.

They could see all of the beautiful buildings,
trees and wildlife of WISHALUZIA,
although everything was looking a
bit charred from the terrible

damage caused by the cat monster. Teeny and the genies flew through colourful clouds, passing beautiful, *magical* birds as they sped towards the palace.

Grant looked down as they got closer to the ornate but cracked turrets and burnt flags.

'That's odd, I can't see the cat monster,' he said, puzzled.

'Teeny, can you fly nearer?' Grant asked, pointing towards the dungeon window.

'Hmm, it's not there! Maybe it saw us coming and we've already scared it away!' said Greta, clapping her hands.

'Hooray!' agreed Dad. 'Now we can just go home and put the kettle—'

But he was interrupted by a humongous **'ROAR!'**

'Wow, Teeny, your roar has really improved!' Dad commented.

'Er, Dad,' said Greta. 'I don't think that roar came from Teeny – look!'

They all turned to where she was pointing

and saw, flying behind them . . .

'THE CAT MONSTER!' Grant shouted.

A little nervous flame appeared from Teeny's rear.

'YIKES! Teeny – fly faster and head up through the clouds. We need to lose him!'

'So much for cats being scared of dogs,' Greta huffed at Grant as Teeny flew up towards the clouds.

CHAPTER 10
THE CHASE!

'I think we lost him!' Grant sighed in relief.

But, a moment later, the cat monster suddenly burst out of a big cloud right next to them, swiping at Teeny. Grant had spoken way too soon!

'What are we going to do?!' shouted
Greta. 'The cat monster was supposed to be
terrified of Teeny, but it doesn't seem the least
bit bothered by him.'

Dad had a think, then whispered into

Teeny's ear. 'Teeny! Remember our loop-the-loop training? It's time to put it into action!'

Teeny nodded.

'Hold on tight, you two,' he said to Grant and Greta, then he counted down . . .

'THREE, TWO, ONE . . . NOW, TEENY!'

Teeny suddenly sped forward, then zoomed high into the air above the clouds, before doing a huge loop-the-loop . . .

Up, over and down again. . .

Now they were behind the cat monster, who looked utterly shocked.

'Do your most ferocious roar, Teeny!' Greta shouted.

Teeny nodded again, closed his eyes, took a deep breath, then let out a terrifying, 'WOOF WOOF ROOOO-OOOAAAAAAAR!' so that he even surprised himself at how loud and scary it sounded.

The cat monster looked worried and sped up as Teeny continued to chase it. 'WOOF WOOF ROOO-OOAR WOOF!' woof-roared Teeny, hot on the cat monster's tail.

The cat monster flew lower towards
WISHALUZIA, weaving
in and out of the tall, fancy
buildings. Then he headed
towards a narrow cave
entrance on a rocky cliff
face below the palace.

'That must be where he's been hiding!' exclaimed Grant. 'Follow him, Teeny!'

Teeny lowered his eyebrows determinedly and focused on the cave entrance. He got closer and closer as he watched the cat monster disappear into it.

'Teeny, watch out! It's too narrow for you – turn round, quick!' Grant shouted.

'It's okay, Grant, watch,' replied his dad. 'TEENY, BARREL-ROLL . . . NOW!'

Teeny nodded again, closing his wings round the genies. Then he twisted his body so it was as small as could be and whizzed sideways into the cave.

CHAPTER 11
WHERE IS THE CAT MONSTER?

'WOOHOOO! Teeny, that was amazing!' shouted Greta, punching the air as Teeny unfurled his wings again.

The cave widened to reveal a dark cavern, lit only by rainbow-coloured fireflies that floated in the air.

'WOW! This place is beautiful,' said Greta as she stared in amazement at all the colours reflecting off the ceiling.

'But where has the cat monster gone?' asked Grant, puzzled.

Teeny landed on the floor of the cave and the four of them had a look around.

'Look! Claw prints!' Grant shouted, pointing to the large cat paw marks on the ground.

'Let's follow them!' they all agreed.

Teeny sniffed around the floor till his nose eventually led them to the entrance of another cave. But this one was so dark that they couldn't see into it.

'We need more light! Look, there are some torches on the walls!' said Grant. And he was right – there were indeed some unlit torches either side of the cave entrance.

'But how are we going to light them?' asked Greta.

'I know,' giggled Dad. 'We need Teeny to do his fire trick!'

Grant and Greta giggled too. Teeny didn't see what was quite so funny.

'Teeny, we need you to breathe fire on to the torches, then we can go into the cave to get the cat monster!' said Grant, handing him the bottle of hot sauce he'd handily brought with him.

Teeny looked puzzled at first, then the penny dropped and he realised what they were asking him to do.

He turned round and the genies moved out of the way as his tail swooshed above them. Then he took a sip of the hot sauce,

concentrated, held his breath, then made a loud, echoey PARP noise. A jet of flame shot across the cave entrance, lighting the torches.

The genies all giggled. Then, abruptly, they stopped giggling as the cat monster appeared in the mouth of the cave, looming over them, its jaws wide and ready to . . .

CHAPTER 12

WHO IS THE CAT MONSTER?!

'HA HA HA! HOO HOO HOO! HE HE HEEEEEE!' The cat monster laughed loudly, pointing at Teeny's bottom. 'I haven't laughed so much in years!' came a very posh-sounding voice from the beast's lips.

Teeny looked embarrassed and put his claws over his bum.

'You . . . you can talk?' asked Grant.

'Of course I can talk,' the cat monster replied.

'But . . . you're a monster! Monsters don't talk – they fly around, scaring genies and setting fire to WISHALUZIA!' added Greta.

'I'm not a monster,' replied the monster, or whatever it was.

'I'm really confused,' said Dad, scratching his head. 'So, you aren't going to eat us or set fire to us?' he asked.

'Not after seeing that hilarious display of flatulent flame!' said the cat monster, who wasn't a monster. 'Absolutely hilarious! Ha ha!' He laughed again. 'Sorry, allow me to explain. Follow me,' he said as he led Teeny and the genies into the cave.

He breathed fire and all the torches along the walls illuminated the inside of the cave. They walked for a few moments before entering a large circular room that had a fireplace, furniture and paintings on the walls. There was even a bed and some books piled high next to it.

'Welcome to my home. Please take a

seat and I'll pop the kettle on,' said the cat monster, gesturing towards a very large chair that was big enough for them all to sit on.

'I don't think it will fit,' Dad replied.

'Not now, Dad!' said Greta as she elbowed him in the side.

'HA HA! Oh, you are a funny bunch!'

laughed the cat monster.

He lit the kettle with his fiery breath then, when it boiled, he poured three small cups of delicious hot chocolate.

'Marshmallows and sprinkles?' he asked the genies.

They all nodded. 'Yes, please!'

'Teeny will just have water, please,' added Grant.

The cat monster poured water into a large bowl before giving it to Teeny. Then he poured himself an even larger saucer of milk and started to lap it up, splashing it all over everyone.

'Oops, sorry,' he apologised. 'I haven't had company for so long I've forgotten my manners. Please do forgive me,' he said, bowing.

As he did so, Grant noticed the crown on top of his head again, its magnificent jewels shimmering in the torchlight.

'How come you wear a crown?' Grant asked him.

'Ah yes, well, I'd better tell you my story. Are you sitting comfortably?'

Teeny and the genies all nodded as they slurped their drinks.

'Then I shall begin . . . ' said the cat monster.

CHAPTER 13
TWiN TROUBLE!

*O*nce upon a time, there were two young genie twins. One was a little princess genie, the other a little genie prince. They lived very happily in a beautiful big palace with their father, the king, and played together each day, running through the palace hallways and round the gorgeous gardens.

'Both genies LOVED to play games. Their favourites included genie hide-and-seek, genie chess, genie musical chairs and genie leapfrog.

'One day, they were having a genie chess tournament and the genie prince beat the genie princess six times in a row. "GENIE MATE!" the prince shouted as he took the princess's last chess piece. This made the princess a little bit angry.

'The next day, they were playing genie hide-and-seek. It was the prince's turn to find the princess, so she went and hid.

"Ninety-nine, ONE HUNDRED . . . COMING, READY OR NOT!" shouted the prince, then went in search of his sister. But, as he was looking for her, he heard the sound of the ice-cream genie outside the palace walls and went to get one, totally forgetting about his sister. He didn't remember that she was still hiding until dinnertime that night. This made the princess very angry.

'The next day was the prince and princess's seventh birthday. "Now, son and daughter,

what would you like for your special day?"
the king asked his children.

'The prince didn't really want anything in
particular, but he did ask if he could have a
pet dragon. The princess really, REALLY
wanted a kitten, but the king said he was
allergic to cats and so she couldn't have one.
The princess thought that her father was
joking and that of course she would get what
she wanted for her birthday; she always got
whatever she wanted because she was a bit
spoilt.

'The king presented the twins with their
gifts. The prince unwrapped his first and

was thrilled to see a cute baby dragon at the bottom of the box. He picked it up and gave it a cuddle. "I'll call him Zob!" He beamed.

The princess then unwrapped her big, beautifully wrapped birthday present, expecting to see a cute little kitten. But, when she took off the lid, there wasn't a real kitten inside the box: there was a fluffy toy kitten instead. This made the princess very, very angry indeed.

"'What on WISHALUZIA is this?" she screamed. She grabbed the toy, threw it at the king, then stomped off to her bedroom in floods of tears.

'The prince, still cuddling his baby dragon, picked up the toy kitten and ran to his sister's room. "Would you like to hug my new dragon to cheer you up?" he asked her.

'This didn't make her feel any better. Instead, the princess stood on her bed, raised her hands and exclaimed, "If I can't have a real kitten, I will turn you into one!" She shouted her magic wishy word, which was,

"ZAGA-ZOOMA-THUNDERBLOOMER!"

Then she shouted, "KITTEN!" and pointed her fingers at the prince . . .

'Lightning bolts shot from her fingers and a huge cloud of red glittery smoke surrounded the prince.

'When the smoke cleared, what do you think the princess saw?'

'Oooh, let me guess!' said Grant. 'Was it a cutesy-wutesy unicorn?'

'Ahem, no,' the cat monster said sternly and carried on telling the story.

'What do you think the princess saw?' he started again.

'Oooh, ooh, let me guess!' said Greta. 'Was it a guinea pig?'

'NO,' replied the cat monster.

'Oooh, my turn!' said Dad. 'Was it a cucumber?'

'NO! IT WAS ME!!!' shouted the cat monster.

'Eh? You turned the prince into a cucumber?'

Dad replied.

'NO, THE PRINCESS turned the PRINCE and the TOY KITTEN and the BABY DRAGON into ME! The princess was so furious that I wasn't a cute little kitten, but a little kitten monster, that she threw me out of the window and I landed in the magical waters surrounding WISHALUZIA.'

'Oh, I get it!' Greta said, leaping into the air. 'You were the little prince and now you're a combination of prince, toy kitten and dragon!'

'Exactly!' the cat monster replied. 'I am Prince Zoodle, the rightful ruler of WISHALUZIA! The wicked Princess

Mizelda transformed me into this monstrous beast and I have been in hiding ever since. I eventually found this empty cave, and I've been concocting a plan to get back my rightful place on the throne!'

'But you're twins, so why should you be on the throne and not Queen Mizelda?' Dad asked.

'I was born two seconds before she was so I am the oldest!' replied the prince.

'What happened to your dad, the king? Can't he help?' asked Greta.

'Father passed away years ago. That's when my sister took over the throne,' he explained.

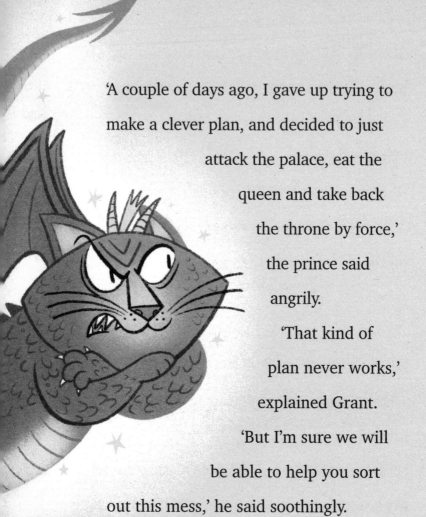

'A couple of days ago, I gave up trying to make a clever plan, and decided to just attack the palace, eat the queen and take back the throne by force,' the prince said angrily.

'That kind of plan never works,' explained Grant. 'But I'm sure we will be able to help you sort out this mess,' he said soothingly.

CHAPTER 14
A NEW PLAN

'First of all, we need to change you back into your real form,' Grant told the prince.

'Believe me, I've tried it all,' Prince Zoodle replied. 'I've tried spells, potions, wishes, everything, but nothing worked. It seems that the only thing that can turn me back into genie form is my horrible sister.'

'Well, let's give it a try, just in case,' Greta suggested. 'I'm sure we can turn you back into Prince Zoodle!' She said her magic wishy word:

'Poodle~parp~ a~pipsqueak!'

and a cloud of pink sparkly smoke appeared.

'WHOOPS!' she giggled.

Greta had turned Prince Zoodle into a noodle by mistake.

'Let me try,' said their dad with a

'Jim-a-jam-a-jumplebumps!'

'DAD!' Grant giggled. 'You've turned him

into an apple strudel!'

'Oops – go on, Grant, you have a go,'

suggested Dad.

Grant stepped forward and shouted,

'Alaka-blam-a-bumwhistle!'

121

This time Prince
Zoodle turned into
a doodle!

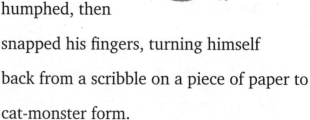

The prince
humphed, then
snapped his fingers, turning himself
back from a scribble on a piece of paper to
cat-monster form.

'See, I told you it's impossible!' he sighed,

licking his paws and wiping his ears.

'Then we shall go and talk to Queen Mizelda

and make her see the error of her ways,' Grant

said firmly. 'TO THE DUNGEONS!'

CHAPTER 15
THE QUEEN OF MEAN!

The magical team of Teeny, Greta, Grant, their dad and Prince Zoodle flew out of the cave and back into the daylight, though it was starting to get dark.

They made their way up to the palace and

landed at the main gate.

'Gosh, I really did make a mess of the place, didn't I?' the prince sighed as a nearby turret crumbled to the ground.

'We can sort that out later. Right now, we need to focus on resolving things with Queen Mizelda first. Come on, it's this way to the dungeons,' Grant told them.

He led them into the palace, through the hallways and down the spiral staircase to the dungeons where Queen Mizelda was lying on the floor, fast asleep and snoring.

'Er, Your Majesty,' Grant whispered. 'Wake up – we have a surprise for you!'

But the queen carried on snoring.

'Your Majesty!' Greta called, slightly louder.

The queen continued to snore, dribble
running down her chin.

'OI, QUEENIE!' shouted the prince really
loudly.

The queen woke up and screamed,

'AAAAAAAAAAAARGH! IT'S THE
MONSTER! GUARDS! GUARDS, HELP
ME! Oh, there
still aren't any
guards, are
there? AAAAAAAAARGH!'

'Oh, calm down. I'm not going to hurt you,' said Prince Zoodle.

'We are just here to sort out a kitty, sorry, tricky situation, Your Majesty,' added Grant.

'Oh, you again. You finally came back, did you?' the queen said in disgust.

'Yes, and I brought my family and my best friend, Teeny, to help,' said Grant, smiling proudly.

'AAAAAAAAARGH! ANOTHER MONSTER!' she screamed as Teeny stepped out from behind the prince. 'Can someone please explain what in WISHALUZIA is going on here?!' the queen demanded.

'Well, why don't we start with the fact that you actually shouldn't be queen, SIS!' the prince replied.

The queen gasped. 'But . . . but . . . it, it can't be you. I thought I'd got rid of you years ago!'

'So you thought! After you turned me into this,' he said, pointing at his wings and tail, 'I have been living underneath the palace, growing bigger and stronger and waiting for the right time to take my revenge!' He loomed over the queen.

'I WAS going to eat you, you know,' the prince said. 'But, fortunately for you, my new friends here persuaded me not to. I still could

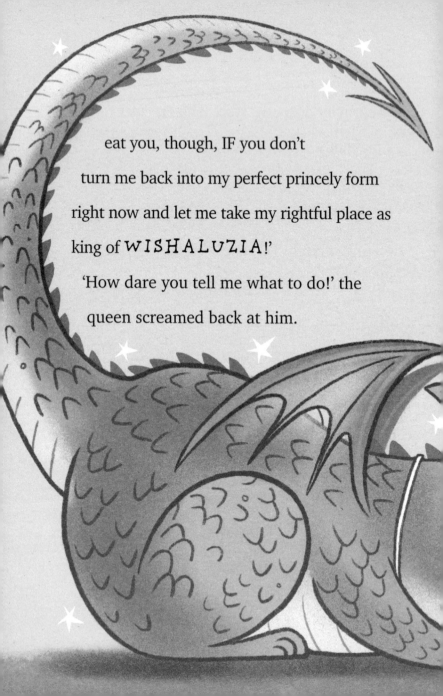

eat you, though, IF you don't

turn me back into my perfect princely form

right now and let me take my rightful place as

king of WISHALUZIA!'

'How dare you tell me what to do!' the

queen screamed back at him.

The prince took a breath, then ROARED
so loudly it nearly blew her hair off!

'All right, all right!' she cried, 'I'll do it. Just
don't eat me!'

'You promise?' Grant asked the queen.

'I promise,' she said.

CHAPTER 16
A MONSTER LIE!

Queen Mizelda raised her hands, said her

magic wishy word,

'ZAGA-ZOOMA-THUNDERBLOOMER!'

and red sparkly smoke filled the dungeon, but

the prince hadn't changed and was still the cat monster.

'Hey! You promised to turn him back!' Greta shouted at the queen. But the queen wasn't listening. Instead, she was GROWING.

'You stupid fools!' she screamed down to them as she grew and grew and grew until she burst out of the dungeons and into the palace grounds. 'Did you really think I would turn my idiot of a brother back into the genie prince so he could rule WISHALUZIA?'

'We did actually,' Grant replied.

'Well, then you are fools! Now bow to your Dragon Queen!' she boomed.

'What a meany! So she was the baddy all along!' Greta humphed.

'Thank you for not eating me, brother, but now I am going to eat YOU, AND your silly little friends!' the Dragon Queen hollered, leaping high into the air. 'I AM GOING TO CRUSH YOU ALL WITH MY **ENORMOUS** BOTTOM, MWAH-HA-HA!'

They all flew out of the way in the nick of time . . . just as the giant Dragon Queen's big bum destroyed what was left of the palace.

'GAAAAAAAH!' she screamed, before flapping her gigantic wings and flying back up into the sky. She cackled as she swooped through the air, breathing fire and roaring. 'I'll get you this time!' she called as she flew towards Grant and the gang with her jaws wide open.

Grant, Greta, Dad, Teeny and the prince flew away as quickly as they could, but it was no use. The Dragon Queen was too fast for them and, in one **ENORMOUS** chomp, she gobbled them up!

CHAPTER 17
I WASN'T EXPECTING THAT!

The Dragon Queen was just about to start chewing everyone when suddenly . . .

'MIZELDA! What ARE you doing?!' an elderly voice shouted.

The queen stopped in her tracks and looked down.

'As your father, I command you to LET THEM GO AT ONCE!' the voice said.

The queen's jaw dropped wide open in shock and the genies, the prince and Teeny all jumped out and flew down to the ground next to . . .

'KING ZANDOR! You're alive! I thought you died eons ago!' exclaimed Grant.

'Yes, that's what my very naughty, selfish daughter, Princess Mizelda, WANTED you to believe. Not only did she turn her brother into a cat monster and throw him out of a window, she also locked me in my lamp and threw me into the dungeons,' he explained.

'Daddy, oh, thank goodness you're safe!' the queen said.

'Stop it, Mizelda! I have had enough of your fibbing. It's time I made everything right again.'

The king clapped his hands and said his magic wishy word:

'ZINGA-ZONGA-ZABRACADOOBEE!'

and a huge plume of purple sparkly smoke surrounded everyone.

The smoke finally disappeared to reveal Prince Zoodle, Princess Mizelda and Teeny in their real forms.

'Ah, that feels better! Thank you, Father,' the prince said, giving his dad a hug.

Princess Mizelda also went to give the king a hug, but he raised his hands to stop her.

'Daughter, it is time you learned your lesson. You cannot behave like this any more – you're grounded, now go to your room!' he said sternly.

'But there AREN'T any rooms – the palace is destroyed, Daddy!' Mizelda replied sarcastically.

The king clapped his hands again and another cloud of purple sparkly smoke twirled round the crumbling remains of the palace, then faded away to reveal the palace and all of WISHALUZIA restored to their original, beautiful form.

'NOW you can go to your room and think about what you've done, Mizelda!' repeated the king to his daughter. And Mizelda sulked off to her room, slamming the door shut behind her.

CHAPTER 18
A ROYAL REWARD!

The next day, there was a huge celebration across WISHALUZIA and crowds gathered in the palace for a very special ceremony. There were multicoloured rainbows, birdsong and beautiful golden

wishing stars twinkling in the sky.

Inside the palace the royal guards played a
fanfare on their trumpets as Grant and Teeny
walked towards King Zandor and Prince
Zoodle in the grand hall.

143

'Grant the genie and Teeny the puppy – we are gathered here today to thank you for saving WISHALUZIA!' announced the king to the crowds of genies, who all cheered.

'Now, young genie – is there a special wish I can grant you as your reward?' the king asked.

'Well, Your Majesty, I would just like to be allowed to live here again and – be with my family,' Grant replied solemnly.

'Why, of course. Your wish is granted.' And the king clapped his hands, said his magic wishy word:

'ZINGA-ZONGA-ZABRACADOOBEE!'

and Grant's dad and sister flew in and gave Grant a huge family hug.

'And, Teeny, what is your special wish? It can be anything your heart desires,' the king said.

Teeny didn't quite understand what the king was saying, but he knew that he was feeling a bit homesick and that he was missing Tilly back on Earth. She hadn't been part of this adventure *or* the excitement on WISHALUZIA, and he really wanted to see her.

Teeny closed his eyes and thought about Tilly, wishing to be with her again.

●

The king seemed puzzled and the palace fell silent.

'Look!' someone shouted from the crowd. 'Up in the sky!'

Everyone looked up to see a bright golden star flying towards them! It was getting nearer and nearer and was so bright everyone had to squint to see what happened next.

The gold star whizzed through the window and whooshed towards the puppy, then, to Teeny's surprise, it picked him up and hovered next to Grant.

'Oh, Teeny, you must have made a wish on this wishing star!' Grant said.

Teeny waved at Grant with a tear in his eye.

Grant, his family and the king waved back
at Teeny, and the star flew off with Teeny
riding on top of it.

'Wait, Teeny! I'm coming with you!'
Grant shouted after him. He quickly flew into
the sky and chased after his best friend.

He eventually caught up with them and
grabbed on to the star
next to Teeny.

Teeny was really excited to see his best friend
and on they flew!

'WHEEEEEEE!'

CHAPTER 19
A STARRY, STARRY NIGHT!

Tilly had just got home from school and was looking for Teeny.

'Where are you, boy?' she called, but there was no reply.

She went up to her bedroom and searched

again, but there was no sign of him anywhere.

Oh no! He's not gone missing again, has he? she thought to herself.

She looked out of the window to see if he was in the back garden, but he wasn't there.

Then, out of the corner of her eye, she saw something shiny in the sky. She looked closer and followed it as it came towards the house.

'TILLYYYYYYYY! Open the window – it's us!' Grant shouted, and Teeny woofed as Tilly quickly opened the window and the wishing stars whizzed into her bedroom.

'WOW, Grant, it's so good to see you!

Where have you two been?' Tilly giggled in amazement.

'Well, it's quite a long story, Tilly. You'd have to read this entire book to find out all the details, but basically we saved WISHALUZIA and everything is wonderful again!' Grant replied as the wishing stars faded and disappeared.

'Oh, Grant! I'm so pleased to hear that,' said Tilly, giving him and Teeny a big welcome hug.

Just then, Tilly saw another star in the sky, then another and another!

'Ha ha! It looks as though you have a few

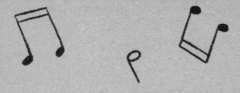

more visitors, Tilly!' Grant giggled.

And he was right because there, flying towards them on more magical wishing stars, was Grant's dad, his sister Greta, King Zandor and Prince Zoodle! The four of them arrived in Tilly's bedroom and landed on her bed. The wishing stars all faded away.

'Hello, Tilly! We heard so much about you and your wonderful planet we just had to pay you a visit! LET'S PARTY!' the king shouted. He clapped his hands and shouted,

'ZINGA-ZONGA-ZABRACADOOBEE!'

Then the music started and a glitter ball and

disco lights appeared!

Everybody laughed and danced. They were all having a wonderfully silly time.

But, mid-bop, Teeny noticed that it was suddenly dark outside and a storm was rapidly brewing as thunder and lightning flashed across the sky.

The music stopped and everyone looked out of the window. There in the distance was another wishing star.

'Oh no! It's MIZELDA!' cried Prince Zoodle. 'What does she want?' he sighed.

The wishing star flew through dark grey clouds, dodging the flashing lightning bolts, and whizzed in through the window.

Princess Mizelda stood before everyone and cackled, 'MWAH-HA-HA-HAA! You thought you could leave without me knowing? NEVER!' she cried.

'Why are you here?' the king asked.

'Well . . . every party needs a cake, so I brought one!' She giggled, and a huge celebratory cake appeared in her hands. 'I had a good long think in my room, Daddy, and you were right – I've been a real rotter and so this cake is an apology for my behaviour,' she said with a hopeful smile.

'Ah, daughter, this is wonderful news!' And the king and Prince Zoodle gave her a forgiving hug.

'START THE MUSIC!' Mizelda shouted and they all began dancing again.

'TILLY! WHAT ON EARTH IS GOING ON IN THERE! TURN THAT MUSIC DOWN!' Tilly's mum shouted, banging on the door.

'Sorry, Mum, I'll turn it down!' she called back.

'I have an idea!' Grant said, a twinkle in his eye, and with an

'Alaka-blam-a-bumwhistle!'

the party disappeared, then reappeared inside

Grant's tea-lamp and the celebration went on

into the night.

Goodnight,

Genie and

Teeny, and well

done for saving

WISHALUZIA!

HOW TO DRAW QUEEN MIZELDA

1 Start with her eyes, eyebrows and mouth.

2 Add an ear and a 'j' shape for her back.

3 Then her pointy nose and a curvy line for her tummy.

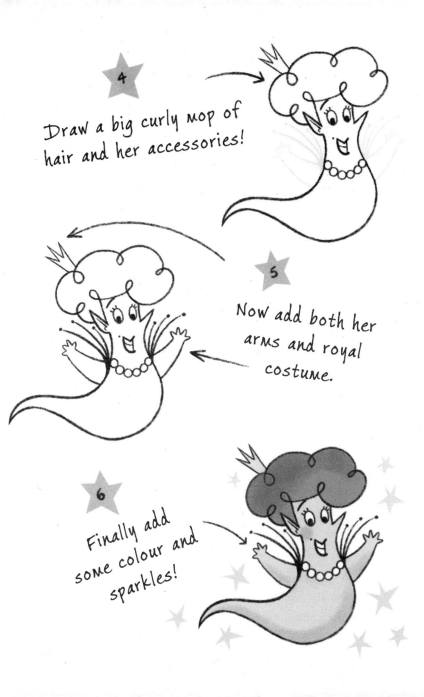

4

Draw a big curly mop of hair and her accessories!

5

Now add both her arms and royal costume.

6

Finally add some colour and sparkles!

STEVEN LENTON is a multi-award-winning illustrator, originally from Cheshire, now working from his studios in Brighton and London with his French bulldog, Big-Eared Bob!

He has illustrated many children's books, including *Head Kid* and *Future Friend* by David Baddiel, *The Hundred and One Dalmatians* adapted by Peter Bently, the Shifty McGifty and Slippery Sam series by Tracey Corderoy, Frank Cottrell-Boyce's fiction titles and Steven Butler's Sainsbury's Prize-winning The Nothing to See Here Hotel series.

He has illustrated two World Book Day titles and regularly appears at literary festivals, live events and schools across the UK.

Steven has his own Draw-Along-A-Lenton YouTube channel, showing you how to draw a range of his characters, and he was in the Top 20 Bookseller Bestselling Illustrator Chart 2019.

The Genie and Teeny series is Steven's first foray into children's fiction and he really hopes you are enjoying Grant and Teeny's adventures!

Find out more about Steven and his work at stevenlenton.com.